RETURN TO OZ

When Dorothy is transformed back to the magical Kingdom of Oz, she finds the Emerald City in ruins, and all its inhabitants turned to stone by the evil Nome King. But Dorothy and her talking hen Billina make some extraordinary new friends – Jack Pumpkinhead, the amazing Gump and the copper man Tik Tok – and they have many exciting adventures before they finally defeat the Nome King and his evil companions, the wicked Princess Mombi and the deadly Wheelers. In the end, Dorothy sees the Emerald City restored to its former glory and is reunited with her old friends, the Scarecrow, the Tin Woodman and the Cowardly Lion, before returning home to her Aunt Em and Uncle Henry on their quiet Kansas farm.

Based on stories by
L. Frank Baum

Based on the motion picture from Walt Disney Pictures
Executive Producer Gary Kurtz
Produced by Paul Maslansky
Written by Walter Murch & Gill Dennis
Directed by Walter Murch

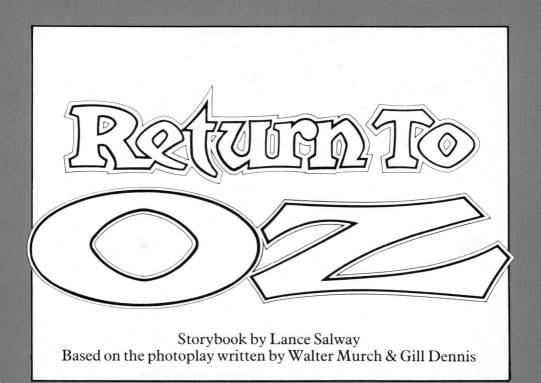

Storybook by Lance Salway
Based on the photoplay written by Walter Murch & Gill Dennis

Hippo Books
Scholastic Book Services Inc.
London

Scholastic Books Services Inc.,
10 Earlham Street, London WC2H 9LN

Scholastic Inc.,
730 Broadway, New York, NY 10003, USA

Scholastic Tab Publications Ltd,
123 Newkirk Road, Richmond Hill
Ontario L4C 3G5, Canada

Ashton Scholastic Pty Ltd, Box 579, Gosford
New South Wales, Australia

Ashton Scholastic Ltd, 165 Marua Road,
Panmure, Auckland, New Zealand

First published by Scholastic Book Services Inc., 1985 by
arrangement with Walt Disney Productions

ISBN 0 590 70420 6

All rights reserved
Made and Printed by Chorley & Pickersgill Ltd, Leeds
Typeset in Plantin by Keyline Graphics

In a small farmhouse in the middle of Kansas, a girl called Dorothy Gale lay wide awake, staring through her bedroom window at the stars scattered across the wide night sky. At the foot of her bed the little dog, Toto, lay fast asleep.

The door opened and Dorothy's Aunt Em tiptoed into the room and sat down on the bed. She was carrying a lantern that cast dancing shadows on the wall.

"Can't you sleep, Dorothy?" she asked. "Had a bad dream?"

Dorothy shook her head.

"It's past one o'clock in the morning," her aunt went on.

There was silence for a moment, and then Dorothy said, "I wish. . ."

"What, precious?"

Dorothy pointed at Toto and laughed.

"I wish I could just put my head on my paws and go to sleep, like Toto."

Aunt Em stroked the girl's forehead and said tenderly, "You will soon, dear. You will soon." Then she tiptoed out of the room and into the kitchen.

Uncle Henry was sitting at the table, reading a newspaper. "She's wide awake," Aunt Em told him. "We've got all the trouble we need without having to worry about Dorothy as well. She's not been herself since that tornado six months ago. All she does is talk about a place called Oz that doesn't exist, and about talking tin men and – and scarecrows." She sat down beside him. "There's nothing else for it, we'll have to get help for her. There's a new doctor in town who says he can cure anything with some sort of electrical machine. I'll take Dorothy to see him tomorrow. Maybe he can help her."

Dorothy was up early the next morning, anxious to see if her pet hen, Billina, had laid any eggs. Billina was easy to find – all

the other chickens on the farm were white. Billina was the only golden hen among them. Dorothy picked her up and stroked her. "Did you lay an egg this morning, Billina?" she asked. "Let's go and look, shall we?"

Dorothy couldn't find Billina's egg anywhere in the farmyard. "Oh dear," she said anxiously. "Aunt Em said that if you don't start laying soon then she'll cook you for supper one night."

But Billina took no notice; she was much too busy pecking at something in the mud. She clawed at it and then tossed it into the air with her beak. It landed near Dorothy, who picked it up. It was a rusty old key, caked with mud.

Dorothy brushed the mud away until she was able to see the key more clearly. It was a most unusual shape – the thumbpiece was in the form of a circle with a diagonal shaft across it. Dorothy traced the circle with her finger, and then the diagonal.

"O. . .Z. . ." she whispered. "Oz!"

Full of excitement, Dorothy ran to find Aunt Em.

"But it's just an ordinary old key," Aunt Em said when Dorothy showed it to her.

"No, it isn't!" Dorothy said. "It's from Oz, Aunt Em. It's proof! They sent it to me!"

"Dorothy, stop it!" her aunt said sharply. "I've told you a hundred times not to mention that place again. It's all in your imagination. I know you don't want to go to the doctor today, but we've got to do something. You haven't slept properly for weeks and you're no help to me on the farm because of it. All you can think of is that place called Oz."

"But my friends there are in trouble, Aunt Em! I just know it!"

"*We're* the ones in trouble, Dorothy," her aunt went on. "We lost our old house in that tornado and we have to get the farm back to rights before winter. Oz isn't real! You only *imagine* that you went there and had adventures. But the new doctor will soon put you right, you'll see. Run along and get ready now or we'll be late."

It was a long journey to town and thunder clouds were beginning to blot out the blue sky by the time Aunt Em and Dorothy arrived at the doctor's elegant house. The door was opened by a tall, severe-looking woman, and then Doctor Worley himself appeared to greet them.

"Good afternoon, Mrs Blue," he said to Aunt Em, and then he smiled at Dorothy. "And you must be Dottie."

"Dorothy," Aunt Em put in quickly.

"Ah yes, Dorothy," smiled Doctor Worley. "Of course." Then he indicated the frowning woman who had opened the door. "This is Head Nurse Wilson," he said. "Well now, Dorothy. Come along to my office and tell me why you've come all this way and what I can do to make you happy."

Doctor Worley led the way to his office, and it wasn't long before Dorothy was telling him all about the adventures she had had in the magical land of Oz. The doctor sat at his desk and listened attentively, glancing every now and then at Aunt Em. In his hands he held the key that Billina had found.

". . . he was made entirely of tin," Dorothy was saying, "even the . . ."

"That's right, Dorothy," the doctor interrupted her. "Now, you mentioned something about a tiger . . ."

"A lion," Dorothy said. "A cowardly lion."

"And could *he* talk, like the scarecrow and the tin man?"

"Oh yes!" Dorothy said excitedly. "He . . ."

"And how did you get back from – from Oz?"

"With my ruby slippers, of course," Dorothy replied.

"Exactly how did they work?"

"Well," Dorothy explained, "you put them on and click the heels three times and say, 'There's no place like home'. But – but I lost them. They fell off on the way back and . . ."

Her voice tailed off and she looked miserably at the doctor. She felt sure that he didn't believe a single word she was saying.

There was a pause, and Doctor Worley cleared his throat and handed the key back to Dorothy. "I know just the thing to cheer you up," he said. He stood up, crossed to a cupboard and opened it. Inside stood a tall gleaming box with a glass door at the top, rather like a grandfather clock. The doctor wheeled the box into the room.

"This is the electical marvel which will make you sleep again," he said. "It will also take away those bad waking dreams you've just been telling me about.

"Will it hurt?" Dorothy whispered.

"Oh no, no, no. Not at all, my dear. It just manages the electric current. The brain is like an electrical machine. Sometimes it produces useless excess currents that cause dreams and delusions. We use this machine to control them."

Dorothy didn't really understand but she said, "Yes, I see." Then Head Nurse Wilson took Dorothy's hand and they went into the hall where Aunt Em said goodbye.

"I must get back to the farm before nightfall," Aunt Em told her. "You do understand, don't you?"

Dorothy nodded. She felt very frighten-

ed, but she tried hard not to show it.

"You must be a good girl and do what the doctor and Head Nurse tell you," Aunt Em went on. "I'll be back to collect you next week."

"She's in good hands," the doctor said.

As soon as Aunt Em had gone, Head Nurse Wilson led Dorothy upstairs to a small bare bedroom. "Stay here until we come and get you," the nurse snapped. "You may take a nap, if you wish."

But Dorothy didn't feel like sleeping. Instead she looked out of the window at the long road which led back to the farm. Then, suddenly, she saw reflected in the glass a fair-haired girl, dressed in white. Dorothy turned round and saw a girl standing just inside the closed door of her room. She was holding a small carved pumpkin head, which she handed to Dorothy.

"This is for you," the girl said. "It's Hallowe'en soon."

"Thank you," Dorothy said.

There was a sudden flicker of lightning followed by a rumble of distant thunder. Dorothy turned quickly to the window, but when she looked back again the girl had gone as mysteriously as she had arrived.

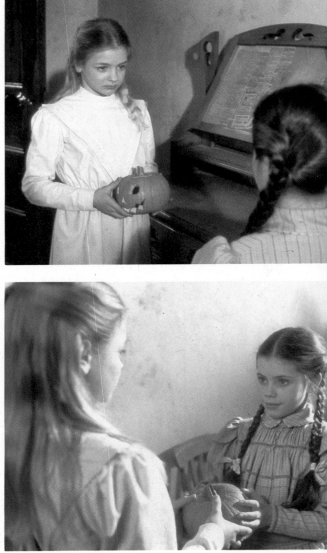

After a while, the door opened and Head Nurse Wilson appeared. Behind her stood some assistants with a trolley.

"Time for you to go for a ride, Dorothy," the nurse said, and the attendants lifted Dorothy onto the trolley. They tied her down with straps round her wrists and ankles, and a studded belt across her middle. Then they pushed her down the passage, the trolley wheels screeching horribly as they went.

Dorothy heard another crash of thunder when they reached the operating room where Doctor Worley was waiting for her.

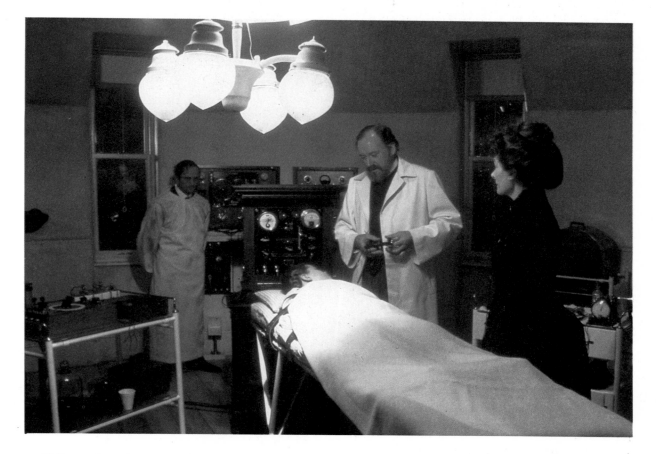

"Now there's nothing at all to worry about," the doctor said. "I'm going to put these muffs over your ears and they'll draw all those unpleasant dreams out of your head. When you wake up you'll never be bothered by them again."

A tangle of wires ran from the ear muffs to the doctor's electrical machine. He placed them over Dorothy's ears and then reached for the switch on the machine.

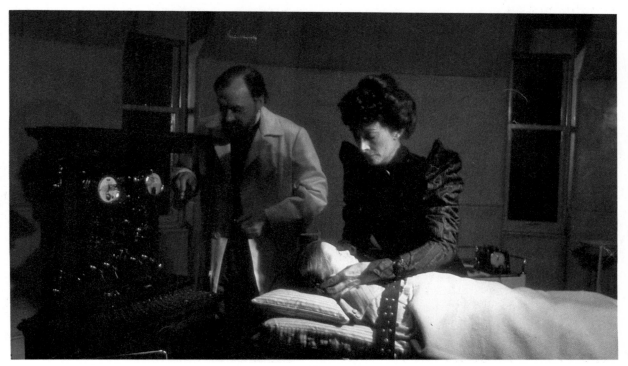

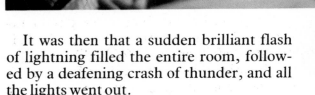

It was then that a sudden brilliant flash of lightning filled the entire room, followed by a deafening crash of thunder, and all the lights went out.

There was silence for a moment, broken only by the heavy drumming of rain on the roof. "Oh dear," Doctor Worley said, and both he and Head Nurse Wilson left the room to investigate.

Dorothy lay where she was in the darkness. Then she suddenly felt the ear muffs being removed and, as another flash of lightning lit up the room, she could see the girl who had given her the pumpkin undoing the straps that tied her to the trolley.

"Quick!" the girl said. "We have to get you out of here!"

She took Dorothy's hand and led her quickly down the stairs to the hall. As they reached the front door, the lights suddenly came on again and the two girls saw Head Nurse Wilson coming towards them with a torch in her hands.

"Run, Dorothy!" the girl shouted. "Run!"

Hand in hand, the two girls raced outside into the driving rain. Behind them rose a noise of shouting and ringing bells. They were being chased! By now the girls were running through bushes and the

18

ground began to slope downwards. Dorothy could hear heavy breathing behind her and the thud of running footsteps. She turned, and saw Head Nurse Wilson behind them, her face twisted in anger. She was gaining on them rapidly.

Suddenly the ground dropped steeply. The girls lost their balance and fell down a deep bank into the rushing water of a swollen river. The current snatched them away from the bank, and Dorothy had a glimpse of Head Nurse Wilson screaming with fury, half in and half out of the river, before she was swept away by the racing water.

Dorothy spun desperately in the river, struggling to stay afloat. Then she saw her friend clinging to the slats of a chicken coop that had been caught in the flood. The girl grabbed Dorothy's hand and pulled her onto the coop.

"It won't hold us both!" the girl shouted, as the flimsy raft sank beneath their weight. "Hold on to it! *Hold on!*"

Dorothy held on to the slats for dear life as the coop plunged and danced on the water. And then, as a flash of lightning lit up the water and the surrounding trees, she saw to her horror that she was alone. Her friend had vanished!

It wasn't long before the rain stopped falling and the sky began to lighten. Dorothy settled herself more securely inside the coop, which was just firm enough to bear her weight.

The lightning and thunder had stopped, and Dorothy could see stars peering from behind the clouds. Then she noticed something strange about the water – the coop was rising and falling, up and down, as though it were floating on waves. And, when the moon appeared and shone on the water, Dorothy realised with amazement that she was indeed at sea, and that there was no land in sight!

At last Dorothy fell asleep. When she awoke, she found that dawn had broken and that the coop was bobbing more gently on the waves. It was then that she heard a strange clucking noise.

"What's that?" Dorothy sat up in surprise.

"I was just trying to lay an egg, that's all," said a sharp little voice.

There, in a corner of the coop, sat a familiar golden hen.

"Billina!" Dorothy said joyfully.

"Who else did you think it was?" Billina said irritably. "I've never been so wet in my entire life. How big *is* this pond anyway?"

"I don't think it's a *pond*," Dorothy began, but when she peered over the side of the coop she saw that last night's sea had shrunk to the size of a small shallow pond.

"What happened to all the water?" she asked, as the pond shrunk even further before her eyes. She turned back to Billina and said, "And when did *you* learn to talk? I thought hens could only cluck."

"So did I," said Billina. "What do you think of my grammar?"

"Very good for a beginner." Dorothy said. "Of course, if we were in the land of Oz your talking wouldn't seem strange at all." And then, as the pond vanished altogether, leaving the coop high and dry in the middle of a vast expanse of sand, she added, "Perhaps this *is* Oz."

"Hmn!" said Billina. "I think I'll have a look round and find some breakfast."

Billina was just about to flutter off the coop onto the sand when Dorothy shouted, "Wait! If we *are* in Oz, then this must be the Deadly Desert." She peered at the innocent-looking sand. It was dotted with rocks which looked as though they might be stepping stones to safety.

"What's the Deadly Desert?" Billina asked.

"It surrounds Oz. If you touch the sand, you turn into dust."

Billina rolled her eyes in disbelief but she didn't object when Dorothy picked her up and jumped onto the first rock. Carefully she made her way, rock by rock, to solid ground.

"There!" Dorothy said, as she put Billina down. "Let's go over to those trees and find some fruit for breakfast. And then we'll go on to the Emerald City and find the Scarecrow. He's the king of Oz!"

As Dorothy set off for the trees, she didn't notice an eye in one of the rocks that blinked, and watched her as she went. . .

When Dorothy discovered that some of the trees grew lunchboxes that contained sandwiches and cake, she *knew* that she was back in Oz at last! She sat down on the grass to share her food with Billina.

"Oh, Billina, I'm so happy!" she said. "Now you'll see that I was telling the truth about the Scarecrow, and the Cowardly Lion, and the Emerald City. . ."

After they had finished eating, Dorothy and Billina walked on into the forest. It was silent and still among the trees and Dorothy's heart sank. Where were her friends? And then she caught sight of something half-buried in the earth.

"It's just a yellow brick," Billina said scornfully.

"Oh no!" cried Dorothy when she saw countless yellow bricks scattered in confusion between the trees. She started to run along the ruined yellow brick road, with Billina fluttering behind her.

Suddenly the forest ended and Dorothy stopped dead, horrified at what she saw. There, across the valley, lay the Emerald City. But where once had been beautiful buildings, covered with jewels, lay mounds of brick and rubble. The Emerald City was in ruins!

Dorothy and Billina picked their way slowly through the ruins of the Emerald City. The few walls and towers that remained standing had been stripped of all their jewels, and were now drab and pitted. Piles of rubble and broken masonry lay everywhere.

23

Dorothy stopped when she saw a sign painted in big sprawling letters on a fragment of wall. "Beware – the – Wheelers," she read out loud.

"What's a Wheeler?" Billina asked.

Dorothy shook her head, and they moved on. Billina fluttered from walls to broken columns as Dorothy clambered over the debris on the ground. It was then that they noticed the statues, hundreds of statues of men and women, standing or lying all around them.

"What are they?" asked Billina.

"They're the people of the Emerald City," Dorothy explained. "They've all been turned to stone."

Dorothy stumbled on through the ruins. She turned a corner and then gasped as she saw an axe raised above her head! But the axe did not move and she recognised her old friend, the Tin Woodman, turned to stone like the rest, frozen in a final act of resistance.

"Is that a Wheeler?" Billina clucked.

"Oh, no," cried Dorothy. "No, it's the Tin Woodman. What's happened? What's happened to everybody?"

She saw the Cowardly Lion a little way off, with his stone teeth bared in a frozen snarl. But there was no sign of the Scarecrow.

Then Dorothy heard a sudden screeching sound and, from behind a statue of a headless women, glided the most peculiar person that she had ever seen. It had the form of a man except that it rolled on all fours. There were wheels on the ends of his arms and legs instead of hands and feet. The wheels screeched horribly as they turned.

"It's a Wheeler!" Billina squawked. "Run, Dorothy, run!"

The Wheeler gave a sharp, wild cry and rolled quickly towards them. As Dorothy ran, she saw more and more Wheelers coming after them on their screeching, squealing wheels. She picked up Billina and darted down a narrow alleyway. It was only when the alley ended in a blank wall that she realised that it was a dead end. She turned to face the Lead Wheeler, who had braked to a halt in a cloud of dust behind her. The other Wheelers filled the alleyway behind him, and more flitted above her head on the rim of the ruins. The air was filled with their gleeful screaming:

"Got you! You're trapped, chicken! Trapped! Trapped! Trapped!"

25

In desperation, Dorothy tried to climb up the alley wall to escape the Wheelers, but the surface was too smooth. It was then that she noticed the outline of a door in the wall, and a keyhole.

As more and more Wheelers filled the alleyway behind her, Dorothy had a sudden brainwave. She pulled the key that Billina had found out of her pocket and tried it in the lock. There was a click, and the door swung open. The Wheelers saw what was happening and surged forward angrily, but they were too late – Dorothy and Billina had darted inside and closed the door behind them.

They found themselves in a dark room of rock. The only light came from the keyhole. Dorothy peered through it and saw the eye of the Lead Wheeler looking at her. "You'll have to come out sooner or later," he howled, "and when you do we'll tear you into little bits and throw you into the Deadly Desert."

"We haven't done anything to you," Dorothy protested.

"Haven't done anything? You picked a lunchbox without permission. And the Nome King doesn't allow chickens anywhere in Oz."

"Who's the Nome King?" Dorothy asked.

"He is the new ruler of Oz," was the reply.

"But the Scarecrow. . ."

For some reason all the Wheelers seemed to find this terribly funny. They all screamed with laughter and rolled away, leaving two of their number to guard the door.

Dorothy turned back into the room and was astonished to see a shape in the dim light. It seemed to be some sort of man.

"Don't be afraid," Billina said. "It's not alive. It's just a heap of old junk."

Dorothy crept closer. The man was about her height but his body was as round as a ball and he was made entirely of copper. There was a plaque on his chest which read: "Royal Army of Oz." On his back was another plaque which gave instructions about winding him up.

"Let's see what happens," Dorothy said.

She turned the keys under the man's arms and stood back.

The man blinked and his copper moustach twitched. And then he spoke: "Good morn-ing, li-ttle girl. Thank-you for res-cu-ing me. Are you Do-ro-thy Gale?"

"Yes, sir," Dorothy said, surprised.

"I am ver-y pleased to meet you. I am Tik Tok, the Roy-al Army of Oz. The Scare-crow told me all about you."

"What's happened to the Emerald City, Mister Tok?" Dorothy asked anxiously. "And where *is* the Scarecrow?"

"I don't know. Every liv-ing thing turned to stone and the Scare-crow locked me in here and told me to wait for you."

"Well," Dorothy said firmly, "the first thing we must do now is get out of here and away from the Wheelers."

"Well," said Tik Tok, "if you keep me wound up, I'll form-u-late a plan."

A short while later, the door opened slowly and Tik Tok peered out. The Wheeler guards were fast asleep, and Tik Tok and Dorothy crept slowly past them. Just as they reached the end of the alleyway, a horde of Wheelers descended on them from all directions.

Tik Tok went into action. His body turned a complete circle as he flailed out at the Wheelers. They were so taken aback by this strange creature that they fled in panic. All, that is, but the Lead Wheeler, who stumbled and fell, and was caught by Tik Tok before he could escape.

"You'll be sorry for this," the Wheeler whined, his eyes rolling with fear. "I'm a terribly fierce person."

"What happened to the Emerald City?" Dorothy demanded. "And who is the Nome King?"

"He's the new ruler of Oz," replied the Wheeler. "He conquered the city and turned everyone to stone."

"But where's the Scarecrow?" asked Dorothy in alarm.

"Gone!" said the Wheeler. "The only peson who knows where he is, is Princess Mombi. She helped the Nome King to conquer Oz."

"Show us where she lives," Tik Tok ordered.

"If I do, will you let me go?" pleaded the Wheeler.

"If you pro-mise to be-have your-self," Tik Tok said grimly.

And the little group set off, Tik Tok holding the Wheeler by his coat tails like a dog on a lead.

Dorothy, Billina and Tik Tok stood outside Princess Mombi's palace, waiting for someone to answer their knock. When no one came, Tik Tok turned the knob and the door swung open. They could hear someone playing a mandolin in the distance and they walked towards the sound through many rooms and up many stairways.

At last they found themselves in a great room panelled entirely with mirrors from floor to ceiling. A beautiful young woman was sitting in the centre, playing upon a mandolin.

"I beg your pardon," Dorothy said politely, "but are you Princess Mombi?"

The woman stopped playing and yawned. "I must put on something more suitable," she said to Dorothy. "Ask your friends to wait here." And she led Dorothy out of the room and into another which was lined with thirty elegant glass-doored cabinets, and one with a mirrored door. One of the glass cabinets was empty but in each of the others was the head of a beautiful woman!

"I think Number Four will do this afternoon," the Princess said and then, to Dorothy's horror, she removed her head

and placed it in the empty cabinet. Then the headless princess walked to cabinet number four, unlocked it with a ruby key, and took the new head from the shelf. This head had black eyes and dark hair, and it suddenly spoke to Dorothy from Mombi's hands. "Well, what do you think?"

"I think it's very beautiful," Dorothy gulped.

"I should think so too," the princess said, as she fitted the new head to her neck. "And who exactly *are* you?"

"I'm Dorothy Gale from Kansas and I want to know what happened to the Emerald City and where the Scarecrow is."

The princess stared at her closely. "The Nome King took the Scarecrow back to his mountain," she said. "You know, I think you'll be rather attractive when you're older. I've a good mind to lock you in the tower until your head is ready and then I'll take it." She leaped forward, seized Dorothy by the wrist, and started to drag her from the room.

Dorothy screamed as loudly as she could, and Billina rushed in from the mirrored room and flew into Mombi's face. "Let her go!" she squawked.

But the princess seized Billina as well. "I'll have *you* fried for breakfast!" she hissed.

Tik Tok had also heard Dorothy's screams and he lumbered towards Mombi as she dragged Dorothy and Billina back into the mirrored room. He raised his arm to strike – and froze. "My ac-tion has run down," he said.

The princess gave an evil laugh and pulled Dorothy and Billina through a mirrored door in the wall. She dragged them up a twisting flight of stairs, which grew narrower and steeper until it ended at a mahogany door with a barred opening at the top. Mombi opened the door, and pushed her captives into the room beyond. Then she slammed the door behind them, and latched it.

Dorothy looked round the room. It was thick with dust and cluttered with old furniture and other strange objects. She crossed to the windows and peered out. Far in the distance, beyond the Emerald City and the Deadly Desert, loomed the Black Mountain of the Nome King.

Dorothy turned back into the room and noticed a figure in a corner. He had a round orange head with a broad grin, but his wooden arms and legs were scattered around the floor. To Dorothy's amazement, the figure spoke: "Who are you?"

"I'm Dorothy Gale from Kansas."

"What *is* it?" snapped Billina. "A man or a melon?"

"A pumpkin, *if* you don't mind," said the figure. "My name is Jack Pumpkinhead. I used to be an ordinary pumpkin until Princess Mombi sprinkled some of her Powder of Life on me and I came alive. Then she grew tired of me and threw me into this room."

"Does she have any more of the magic powder?" Dorothy asked, a plan forming in her mind.

"Yes," said Jack. "She keeps it downstairs in cabinet number thirty-one."

"I've an idea," said Dorothy. "But first we must put you back together again and rescue Tik Tok."

Jack's wooden fingers were so long that he was able to stick them through the barred opening in the door and lift the latch on the outside. He and Dorothy crept downstairs to the mirrored room.

Tik Tok was standing exactly where they had left him. There was no sign of Princess Mombi. Dorothy tiptoed across to the copper man and wound him up. Then she introduced him to Jack.

Meanwhile, in the tower room, Jack and Tik Tok were busy constructing a most curious creature: it had a sofa as a body, and other bits and pieces were lashed to it.

"We need a head," Tik Tok said.

Jack looked round the room and saw, hanging over a mantlepiece, the head of an animal that looked like a greenhorned camel.

"What's that?" Billina asked in disgust, as Jack lifted it down.

"It's a Gump," he said, "and it'll do very nicely." He tied the head to one end of the sofa.

"I'm going to find the Powder of Life," Dorothy said. "While I'm away, go back to the tower room and make a raft for us to fly away on. Use anything you can find but make sure that it has a head so that it can see where it's going."

Jack and Tik Tok went back up the stairs. Dorothy crossed the mirrored room and opened a door. It led into Mombi's bedroom. The princess was lying asleep on the bed. Dorothy tiptoed past her towards the cabinet room, hoping that Mombi wouldn't wake up.

Downstairs, in the cabinet room, Dorothy was staring at all the heads asleep in their glass boxes. Cabinet number thirty-one had a mirrored door and so she couldn't see inside it. It was locked. Where was the key?

And then Dorothy remembered. A blood-red ruby key was hanging on a black ribbon round the wrist of the sleeping Mombi. Dorothy would have to take it without waking her up!

Hardly daring to breathe, Dorothy crept back to the bed where Mombi lay. The princess was covered by blankets but luckily the hand carrying the ruby key was lying on top. Dorothy pulled the ribbon gently from Mombi's wrist and darted back into the cabinet room. The princess did not wake.

Dorothy inserted the ruby key into the lock of cabinet number thirty-one. She held her breath as the lock clicked and the door swung open. But what she saw inside made her gasp in horror. A hideous head with hair like snakes was lying there asleep. It was Mombi's original head! Beside it lay her charms and spells, including a box labelled "Powder of Life".

As carefully as she could, Dorothy reached into the cabinet for the box but, as she touched it, the horrible head suddenly woke up. The eyes shot open and the awful mouth snapped at Dorothy's hand. The little girl snatched the box of powder and slammed the cabinet door. The head immediately began to wail, a terrifying unearthly noise that was soon taken up by the other thirty heads behind their glass doors.

Dorothy turned and ran for her life into Mombi's bedroom. The headless princess was sitting up in bed. She jumped out and tried to stop Dorothy but without a head she couldn't see her. Dorothy ran on into the mirrored room and back up the tower stairs. Below and behind her, the heads continued to wail.

36

Jack and Tik Tok were putting the finishing touches to their remarkable creature. They had tied palm leaves on the sides to act as wings. Dorothy ran to the sofa and dusted it liberally with the Powder of Life.

"Don't forget the head," said Jack.

Dorothy dusted the strange horned head, and they all stepped back to see what would happen. But nothing did; there was no movement at all. Then the hideous wailing below them grew louder and louder. Mombi had rescued her horrible head and was now climbing the stairs. There was no time to be lost.

Then, when they had almost given up, the Gump's green wings started to flap, raising a great cloud of dust. The sofa, which was the Gump's body, began to clatter and dance on the floor.

"Quick, climb on!" Dorothy shouted, and they all climbed onto the Gump as it began to lurch across the floor.

The door burst open and Mombi's hideous head appeared. The Gump took one terrified look at her and flapped his wings as hard as he could. A great gust of air filled the room; furniture was flung aside and curtains billowed in the wind as the great window was blown open.

Mombi moved towards them like a horrible black bat as the Gump flew clumsily towards the open window. He crashed through the balustrade outside and began to plummet down to the ruins of the Emerald City below.

stairs and out into the night, her robes streaming behind her. Several Wheelers were curled up asleep at the base of a column. Mombi kicked them awake, and pointed upwards at the Gump, silhouetted against the moon.

"Follow them!" Mombi screamed. "And don't come back without them!"

The Wheelers immediately set off in pursuit, yelping and baying like unearthly hounds.

Dorothy and her friends clung to the Gump for dear life as, just in time, he pulled out of his dive and cleared the ruins with inches to spare. Then he began to soar upwards, away from the ruined city. Dorothy looked back and saw Mombi screaming with rage at the window of the palace. She smiled to herself with relief as the Gump flew on across the night sky.

Back at the palace, Princess Mombi slammed the window so hard that the glass shattered. Then she stormed down the

The Gump sailed on through the night. The silence was broken only by the swishing of the Gump's leafy wings, and by the baying of the pursuing Wheelers on the ground below.

"This is all a very great mistake," Jack said gloomily. "Perhaps it would have been better to end my days as pumpkin pie after all."

"The best thing to do is to keep fly-ing un-til dawn," said Tik Tok. "Then we may be able to find a safe place to land."

"Like Kansas," muttered Billina to herself.

Dorothy curled up in a corner. "I'm feeling awfully tired," she yawned.

"You get some sleep," Jack said. "Tik Tok and I will keep watch."

In the forest beneath, the Wheelers screeched on in pursuit, their flashing eyes fixed on the lumbering shape in the sky above them. Jack peered down at them. "Can't you go any faster?" he asked the Gump.

"Not unless one of you jumps off," the Gump said grimly.

Then, suddenly, the treetops gave way to desert – the Deadly Desert! Most of the Wheelers were so intent on watching the Gump that they didn't notice that the trees had disappeared. They cried out in terror as they toppled onto the sand and began to sink in. Then, in an instant, they vanish-ed, turned into sand themselves. The Lead Wheeler was one of the few who managed to stop in time. He shook his wheels in rage as the Gump sailed on above his head.

Dawn was breaking when Dorothy was suddenly woken by shouting from Jack and squawking from Billina. "What's hap-pening?" she asked.

"One of the cords has bro-ken," said Tik Tok. "I'm try-ing to hold the Gump to-geth-er."

"Oh no!" shouted Dorothy. They were flying now through dense fog, and she held on for dear life as Jack and Tik Tok tried to tie the broken cord. But then another

rope began to split and unwind, and Dorothy lost her grip altogether as the Gump began to come to pieces.

"Help!" screeched the Gump. "I'm coming apart."

"Abandon ship!" squawked Billina.

And then they were all tumbling through the fog – the sofa, Tik Tok, Jack's body, Billina, Jack's head, Dorothy. They fell down into the darkness. . . .

One by one, Dorothy and the others landed on a snow-covered mountain ledge. She wasn't hurt by the fall and neither was Billina, who fluttered down beside her like a feather duster with no handle. Tik Tok and the Gump's head landed on a snow drift, followed by Jack's body. His head followed a fraction of a second later and landed squarely on his pointed neck – upsidedown and back to front!

"Is everybody all right?" Dorothy asked breathlessly.

"I'm all *wrong* somehow," Jack muttered.

Dorothy put his head on properly and then helped Tik Tok to his feet. The copper man's helmet was badly dented but otherwise he was all in one piece.

"Where are we, anyway?" Billina asked, staring up at the dark mountain which rose up to the sky behind them.

"The Nome King's mountain," murmured Dorothy and began to shiver with cold.

"Just a minute," Billina said anxiously. "Didn't the Wheelers say that the Nome King doesn't like chickens?"

"Yes, they did," said Dorothy. "What on earth are we going to do with you?"

"I know," said Jack. "She can hide inside my head."

Once Billina had been safety tucked away inside Jack's hollow pumpkin head, the others set about putting the Gump together again. None of them noticed the face that appeared in the rock wall behind them, a face that watched them work for a moment or two before disappearing. The face reappeared moments later in a different part of the mountain, deep underground in the rocky domain of the Nome King.

"What *was* that noise?" thundered a dark voice.

"Dorothy Gale, Your Majesty," the stone face whispered. "She has escaped from Mombi and crossed the Deadly Desert. Now she is on our mountain with a very small army."

"She is more powerful than I thought," the Nome King said thoughtfully. "But where is the chicken?"

"There is no sign of it," replied the face. "Shall I take care of them with a slight avalanche?"

"No," the Nome King said after a moment's thought. "They might provide me with some amusement. . ."

Meanwhile, on the mountain ledge high above, the Gump had been reassembled – more or less – and they heard a loud booming voice that seemed to come from all around and beneath them.

"Tell me who you are and why you have come to my kingdom."

"It's the Nome King," Tik Tok whispered to Dorothy.

She stepped forward bravely. "My name is Dorothy Gale," she said, "and these are my friends. We have come to ask you to release the Scarecrow from captivity and to restore the Emerald City."

There was a sudden movement in the rock and, all at once, the huge stone face of the king appeared in the cliff face, in the way that faces can sometimes be seen in clouds. His appearance was frightening but Dorothy was encouraged by the warmth in his voice.

"Do you want me to give the Scarecrow back?" the king asked.

"Yes, Your Majesty," Dorothy replied.

"And if I don't?"

"Then our army will conquer you, and force you to release him."

"Army?" The Nome King sounded bewildered. "What army?"

In reply, Tik Tok come noisily to attention, and saluted smartly.

The Nome King started to chuckle, a chuckle that grew into a laugh. He laughed and laughed until he began to choke and cough. The cough grew louder and louder and then, without any warning, the rock opened beneath Dorothy's feet and she was sucked down into the mountain. The others watched in horror as Dorothy fell away from them into the darkness. Down into the

43

mountain Dorothy plunged, spinning and sliding at a tremendous speed, falling through the rock as though it were water. As she fell, the Nome King's voice thundered in her ears:

"All the world's metals and precious stones are made here, in my kingdom. They are made by my Nomes for *my* amusement. Those jewels in the Emerald City belonged to me. I only took what was mine by right."

Dorothy was falling now in a brilliant cascade of emeralds. She twisted and spun in darkness as the Nome King boomed: "Your friend, the Scarecrow, is a thief. I took him prisoner to teach him never to steal from me again."

Then Dorothy emerged from darkness into an enormous rocky cavern, studded with glittering crystals. She slid across the polished floor and came at last to a stop. The Nome King gazed at her from the rock wall, impassive and slightly amused.

"Where *is* the Scarecrow?" Dorothy demanded. "What has happened to him?"

"I have transformed him into a beautiful ornament for my palace."

"But he didn't steal the emeralds!" Dorothy shouted. "The emeralds were already in the city when he arrived." And then she burst into tears.

The Nome King seemed suddenly to

shrink to human size when he saw Dorothy's distress. "Now then, don't cry, Dorothy Gale from Kansas. I didn't realise that the Scarecrow meant so much to you. What can I do to cheer you up? I know. You and your friends can play a little game."

He paused, and suddenly Tik Tok, Jack and the Gump spun into the room beside her.

"You'd risk anything to get the Scarecrow back, wouldn't you?" the Nome King went on, and, when Dorothy nodded, he told them all the rules of the game. "One by one you will go and inspect my ornament collection. Each of you has three chances to guess which ornament is really the Scarecrow. If you touch the right object and say the word 'Oz' at the same time, then the Scarecrow will be restored and may leave the palace. Does that sound fair?"

The four friends put their heads together. "We've no choice," said Tik Tok. "He's a ver-y pow-er-ful mag-ic-ian." The others agreed.

Dorothy turned back to the king. "All right," she said. "We accept."

"Good," said the Nome King. "The sofa can go first."

Part of the rock wall slid aside to reveal a passageway beyond, and the Gump disappeared from view. The others settled down to wait. After a few minutes there was a sudden crack of thunder and a flash of blue light.

"What was that?" asked Jack in alarm.

The Nome King didn't answer. Instead he said, "Next!" and the rock door opened once more.

"But where's the Gump?" Dorothy asked.

"He's been turned into an ornament," said the Nome King. "He failed to guess correctly and so he too has become part of my collection."

"But that's not fair!" Dorothy protested. "You didn't tell us about that!"

"You didn't ask!" the king replied.

"Your turn now, Pumpkinhead."

Jack turned to Dorothy and she put her arms around him. "Be careful, Jack," she said, and added in a whisper, "And you too, Billina." She watched sadly as Jack vanished down the passage.

Minutes later there came another crash of thunder and a flash of blue light. "Now it's your turn, Army of Oz," the Nome King said.

Tik Tok looked at Dorothy. "Good-bye, Do-ro-thy. Don't worry a-bout me. I will think of a way to guess cor-rect-ly."

She waved as Tik Tok walked down the long stone tunnel and then she turned to face the Nome King. He had now become less rocklike than before, and looked almost human as he sat on a throne of granite formed from the wall.

"Did you really come all this way just for the scarecrow?" he asked.

"Yes," Dorothy replied.

"Are you sure you didn't come for these?" He pointed at his feet.

"You're wearing my ruby slippers!" she gasped.

"No, no," said the king. "They're *my* ruby slippers now. They helped me to

46

conquer the Emerald City." He paused as a servant of Nome entered the room and whispered something in his ear. "Oh dear," he went on, "it seems that your Army has stopped guessing. He's standing perfectly still in the middle of the room."

"His clockwork must have wound down," said Dorothy.

"Well, why don't you go in and wind him up? Then you can stay there and guess for yourself." The Nome King waved a hand, and the curtain of rock was drawn aside once more.

Dorothy stared at the passageway, gathering her courage. Then she walked firmly through the doorway and down the tunnel that lay beyond. At the end of the passageway, a stone staircase led to a series of magnificent rooms filled with the Nome

King's treasures. Dorothy wandered in amazement through room after marble room containing beautiful ornaments of every description: vases of coral and crystal, bowls of porcelain and ivory, statues of ebony and alabaster. Dorothy was dazzled by the sparkle of jewels and precious stones and by the gleam of gold and silver.

She found Tik Tok standing in the centre of the third room. To her surprise, she discovered that his clockwork mechanism was perfectly tight. "What's the matter?" she asked. "Why did you stop?"

"Ssh!" whispered Tik Tok. "It was my way of get-ting you here. I have an i-dea that may save us. I have one guess left. If I guess wrong-ly, you can see what I'm changed in-to and it may give you a clue. Ready?"

Dorothy nodded. Tik Tok put his hand on a small yellow vase and said: "Oz!"

He disappeared immediately. There was a flash of blue light and a crack of thunder, and Dorothy was left alone in the magnificent room.

She looked around her. There was no way of telling which ornament was Tik Tok. She touched a silver bowl and said timidly, "Oz!" There was a distant roll of thunder but nothing else happened. Two guesses left. Then she touched an ornamental crystal and said the magic word again. All she heard was a roll of thunder, somewhere far away. "One guess left," Dorothy said to herself. She walked slowly towards a mantlepiece that was crowded with small objects. A tiny brass bird caught her eye and she reached towards it. Then she changed her mind and touched instead a green pincushion that was lying beside it. She closed her eyes tightly and said: "Oz!"

When she opened her eyes, she saw the Scarecrow sitting on the mantlepiece, his eyes round with astonishment. "Dorothy!" he cried.

"Oh, it's you!" she said with delight as he jumped down and hugged her. "How wonderful to see you! But there's no time to be lost. How can we rescue the others?"

"I don't know," the Scarecrow said. "I don't even know which ornament I was."

"You were green!" Dorothy shouted. "You were a green pincushion. Perhaps people from Oz turned into green ornaments. You start looking over there."

The Scarecrow crossed to a shelf crowded with small objects. Nothing there. Then he turned to a nearby sideboard and gave a shout. Dorothy ran over to him, and he pointed at a green inkwell. Dorothy touched it and said: "Oz!"

48

49

Immediately the Gump appeared, much to the astonishment of the Scarecrow, who had never seen him before and didn't quite know what to make of him.

"Look for green objects, quickly!" said Dorothy. "We still have to find Jack, Billina and Tik Tok."

They raced through the rooms, searching for anything that was coloured green. Then, suddenly, a strange trilling noise began and grew steadily louder. The ornaments were vibrating on the shelves and, as the shaking grew stronger, one or two objects toppled to the floor and broke. Dorothy watched in terror as the floor began to split and break, and then she backed away as the Nome King's gigantic rock head forced its way through the floor, filling the far end of the room and scattering ornaments everywhere.

The Scarecrow was just in time to catch a green porcelain vase before it smashed on the floor. Dorothy ran across to him, touched the basket and said: "Oz!" Suddenly, instead of a porcelain ornament, the Scarecrow found that he was holding Jack Pumpkinhead in his arms!

50

"Stop! Stop!" bellowed the Nome King in a thunderous voice.

"We haven't finished guessing," Dorothy said bravely. "You promised. . ."

"I'm tired of playing games," the Nome King boomed. "I'm tired of you all!"

Dorothy and her friends turned and ran through the debris towards a nearby doorway. But it collapsed before they could reach it, and the walls of the room were shattered by huge, ugly Nome faces which emerged from the rock, blocking their escape. They turned to face the Nome King, knowing that they were trapped.

The Nome King laughed, picked Jack up by his heels and lifted him up to his mouth as if to swallow him.

"*No!*" Dorothy screamed.

And then the Nome King stopped, transfixed by a sound that seemed to terrify him.

"Cluck-cluck! Cluck-cluck!"

It was Billina, still hidden inside Jack's hollow pumpkin head.

The Nome King was paralyzed with fear, and there was a gasp of horror from the other Nomes. "A chicken!" they hissed.

An egg appeared in Jack's grinning mouth. It teetered for a moment on the edge and then tumbled straight into the king's mouth. He snapped his jaws closed but it was too late – he had swallowed the egg!

"An egg!" the other Nomes hissed in horror. "Poison! Poison! Poison!"

For an instant there was silence and then pandemonium erupted as the Nomes fled the room in a gigantic cloud of dust, leaving their king alone and abandoned.

"Don't – don't you know that eggs are poison?" the Nome King moaned. He set Jack gently back on the floor, and disappeared from view as a flash of lightning filled the room, followed by a deafening crash of thunder. And then there was blackness and silence.

As the dust and smoke slowly began to clear, light drifted back into the room. Dorothy peered through the gloom, looking for any sign of the Nome King. But there was only a great pile of broken stone where she had last seen him. And then, as she looked more closely, Dorothy caught sight of something red gleaming in the rubble. The ruby slippers! She stepped carefully over the stones and picked up the shoes. They were hers again at last!

The ground suddenly began to shake and huge slabs of masonry started to fall from the ceiling. Pillars toppled to the floor like falling trees, and ornaments cascaded from the shelves in a shower of broken glass and smashed porcelain.

Dorothy tore at the laces of the shoes she was wearing as her friends clustered round

her. "Hurry, Dorothy, hurry!" Billina clucked anxiously. At last one shoe was off but Dorothy was having trouble with the laces of the other. The light began to flare and dim, and a hideous rumbling noise could be heard deep beneath the earth.

At last Dorothy managed to get her second shoe off and, she did so, the room began to rock from side to side. It felt as though they were on a giant seesaw. Quickly Dorothy slipped on the ruby slippers and took a deep breath.

"I wish all of us from Oz to return there safely!" she said.

And then she clicked her heels.

A dense mass of smoke and fire filled the room as Dorothy and her friends vanished from sight. Before they knew exactly what had happened, they found themselves on a high grassy hill. They stared at each other in astonishment as they picked themselves up.

Dorothy looked round. There, in the distance, lay the ruins of the Emerald City. She said firmly, "I command all the emeralds to be returned to the Emerald City, and everyone who was turned to stone to be restored to life." And she clicked her heels.

At her words a rushing wind sang through the leaves of the nearby trees, and summer lightning played gently in the dark evening sky. As Dorothy watched, the ruins began to glow and then shimmer with an unmistakably green light. And, as they watched, the friends saw the city spring back to life before their eyes, the domes and towers gleaming with jewelled radiance.

Dorothy turned to the others, her eyes shining with delight, until she realized that someone was missing. "Where's Tik Tok?" she asked in alarm.

"We never found him," the Scarecrow said sadly. As he spoke, they heard the distant roar and rumble of a huge underground explosion.

The friends looked at each other in dismay. Their copper companion, the brave and noble Army of Oz, had fallen in battle and been lost forever.

Dorothy's eyes filled with tears. "Oh, Tik Tok," she said.

Billina, perched on the Gump's antlers, suddenly started clucking. There, swinging gently from a horn was a beautiful medal, edged with emeralds.

"Where did you get that?" the chicken asked.

"Get what?" replied the Gump, looking bewildered.

And then Jack noticed the medal, too. He picked it off the antler and showed it to the others.

"It must have fallen on to my horns in the ornament collection," the Gump said.

They all stared at the medal. It was made of bright polished copper. Could it be. . .? Dorothy reached to touch it, afraid to say anything in case it turned out to be just a medal after all.

"Go on, Dorothy," the Scarecrow said gently.

"*Oz!*" she said firmly, and closed her eyes tightly.

When she opened them again, Tik Tok was standing in front of her.

Dorothy squealed with delight and flung her arms round him, hugging him tightly. "Oh, you're back!" she said. "You were enchanted but it's all right now. *Everything's* all right!"

That night there was a great celebration in the Emerald City in honour of the coronation of the Scarecrow as King of Oz. The streets blazed with light, and fireworks sparkled in the dark sky, as a colourful procession wound its way through the jubilant, brightly-dressed crowds.

Dorothy and her friends led the procession. She rode on the back of the Cowardly Lion who, like the Tin Woodman and the rest of the people of Oz, had been restored to life. The Scarecrow walked by her side with the Tin Woodman, and they were followed by Billina, perched like a princess on a litter. The key she had found in Kansas hung from her neck on a shining cord. Tik Tok strode along behind her, his round body gleaming like polished gold, and the Gump's head was mounted proudly on the front of a chariot that followed. At the end of the procession rolled a cage in which Mombi crouched, scowling and helpless. Dorothy had removed her magic powers.

At last the procession reached the hall of the castle and the coronation began. The Scarecrow took his place on the throne and

Dorothy raised her hand as a signal for the crowd to fall silent. She picked up the crown and was just about to place it on the Scarecrow's head when he cried: "Wait!"

"What's the matter?" asked Dorothy.

"I was never meant to be king," he replied sadly. "I've got the brains for it, but not the heart."

"But who is to rule if you won't?"

"You."

"Me?" Dorothy asked in amazement.

"Yes," replied the Scarecrow. "Stay here and rule over us, Dorothy. Be the Queen of Oz."

"Yes! Yes! Stay!" the crowd shouted joyfully.

Dorothy waited until the noise died down and then said, "You're the best friends anyone's ever had. But I have to go back home. I'm sure that Aunt Em and Uncle Henry will be worried about me."

"And Toto, too," Billina reminded her.

"Oh dear," said Dorothy. "I'd forgotten about Toto. I'll have so much to tell him about what's happened and all the wonderful people I've met."

Then Billina suddenly called out, "Look there! In that mirror!"

Silence fell as Dorothy walked over to the nearby mirrored wall. There, where her reflection ought to have been, stood another girl, dressed in magnificent robes of silken gauze that floated round her like a cloud. Dorothy recognised her at once – she was the girl who had rescued her from the doctor's house in Kansas and who had been lost in the river!

"Help me step through the glass, Dorothy," the reflection said.

Dorothy touched the surface of the mirror and the reflected fingers rose to meet her. The glass rippled and shimmered and the reflection stepped out of the mirror as though it wasn't there.

"You're so beautiful!" Dorothy breathed. "Who are you?"

"I am Ozma," the girl said, "Queen and rightful ruler of Oz. Mombi enchanted me into a mirror, but I forgive her now that Dorothy has punished her by removing her magical powers."

The crowd erupted with joy as Ozma sat down upon the throne and the Scarecrow lowered the crown on to her head.

Then Dorothy took off her ruby slippers and laid them at Ozma's feet. "Please put

these on," she said, "and wish me back to Kansas."

"On one condition," Ozma smiled, as she put on the shoes. "If you ever wish to return to Oz, I will make it possible."

A mist began to rise gently in the room as Dorothy's friends gathered round her.

"Goodbye, Dorothy," said Billina.

"Aren't you coming back with me?" Dorothy asked in surprise.

"Oh no," the hen said. "It's much more exciting here."

The mist grew thicker and thicker and Dorothy called out, "Oh no! Not yet, not so soon. I haven't said goodbye properly. . ."

The mist wrapped itself around her, and hundreds of voices sounded in her ears: "Goodbye, Dorothy, goodbye!"

Dorothy waved and called out, "Oh, I love you all! I'll never forget you! Never! Goodbye!"

Lights glimmered and flashed and then dimmed as the mist carried her away into darkness.

When Dorothy opened her eyes, she didn't know where she was at first. Then she sat up and saw that she had been lying on a muddy river bank.

A dog barked in the distance. It was a friendly bark, a bark that Dorothy recognised. . .

"Toto!" she called.

The little dog suddenly appeared and rushed joyfully towards her. He was followed by Uncle Henry who fell on his knees beside her and pulled her into his arms.

"Oh, Dorothy," he said. "Thank goodness we've found you. We'd almost given up hope." Then, "She's here!" he called over his shoulder to the search party of farmers and their sons who were running towards them.

Uncle Henry wrapped Dorothy in a blanket and carried her to the road where Aunt Em was waiting in their buggy.

It wasn't long before Dorothy was back in the familiar farmhouse, in the warmth

and safety of her bedroom.

"There was a dreadful storm," Aunt Em was telling her, "and Doctor Worley's clinic was struck by lightning and burned to the ground. Everyone was rescued except the doctor himself. He went back in to save his machine. We couldn't find *you* anywhere. I can't think what possessed me to leave you there in the first place." She wiped her eyes on her apron.

"Never mind, Aunt Em," Dorothy said. "I'm back home now." She crossed to her dressing table and looked idly in the mirror.

There, where her reflection ought to have been, stood Ozma. She was smiling at Dorothy, and holding Billina in her arms. Dorothy gasped in wonder and called out, "Aunt Em! Aunt Em! Come and look!"

"What is it, dear?" said Aunt Em.

The reflection put her finger to her lips and shook her head gently.

"It's all right," Dorothy called quickly. "There's nothing here. Just my reflection!"

"It's nice to be back in your own room, isn't it?" said Aunt Em. "Now stop playing with that mirror and go outside and play. It's too nice a day to stay inside."

Dorothy hugged her aunt and then called to Toto. Together, the little girl and her dog ran outside into the sunshine.

61